D0382252

LITTLE, BROWN AND COMPANY
New York ↭ Boston

Little, Brown and Company

Hachette Book Group USA
1271 Avenue of the Americas, New York, NY 10020
Visit our Web site at www.lb-kids.com

First Edition: January 2006

Library of Congress Cataloging-in-Publication Data

Bang, Molly.
In my heart / Molly Bang.—1st ed.
p. cm.
Summary: Parents describe how their child is always in their hearts, no matter where they are or what they are doing.
ISBN 0-316-79617-4
[1. Parent and child--Fiction.] I. Title.
PZ7.B2271In 2005
[E]—dc22
2003027819

10 9 8 7 6 5 4 3 2 TWP Printed in Singapore

The illustrations for this book were done in watercolor and collage, with some imagery created in Adobe Photoshop. The text was set in Tapioca, and the display type was hand-lettered by Molly Bang.

Emily
To
CHARLIE!
MONIKA
Jessie

You know how every morning,
I put on my shoes and coat, kiss you good-bye,
And walk out the door?
Well, just as I'm leaving, I feel something in my heart.
I look inside,
And what do you think I find?

ou!
Right here in my heart.

When I'm standing with other people
waiting for the bus and

When I'm sitting by myself reading the paper

nd when I take off my coat

and begin
doing my
work,
ou're in my heart. Plenty of room for YOU here!

nd when I'm talking

or eating

or writing

or watching

Or when I'm just listening to the sounds all around me,
You are still
in my heart,
right here.
I can't go anyplace without you!

And when you—yes, it's your turn now—
When you put on your mittens and your coat

And when you stand with other people waiting for the bus

And when you're talking

or eating

or playing

or watching,

You're in my heart then too, all the time.

what about when you're singing or painting or throwing a ball,

Or when you're building a castle or **S**itting on the potty,
Or when you're **L**ying down listening to the sounds all around you,
How about then?

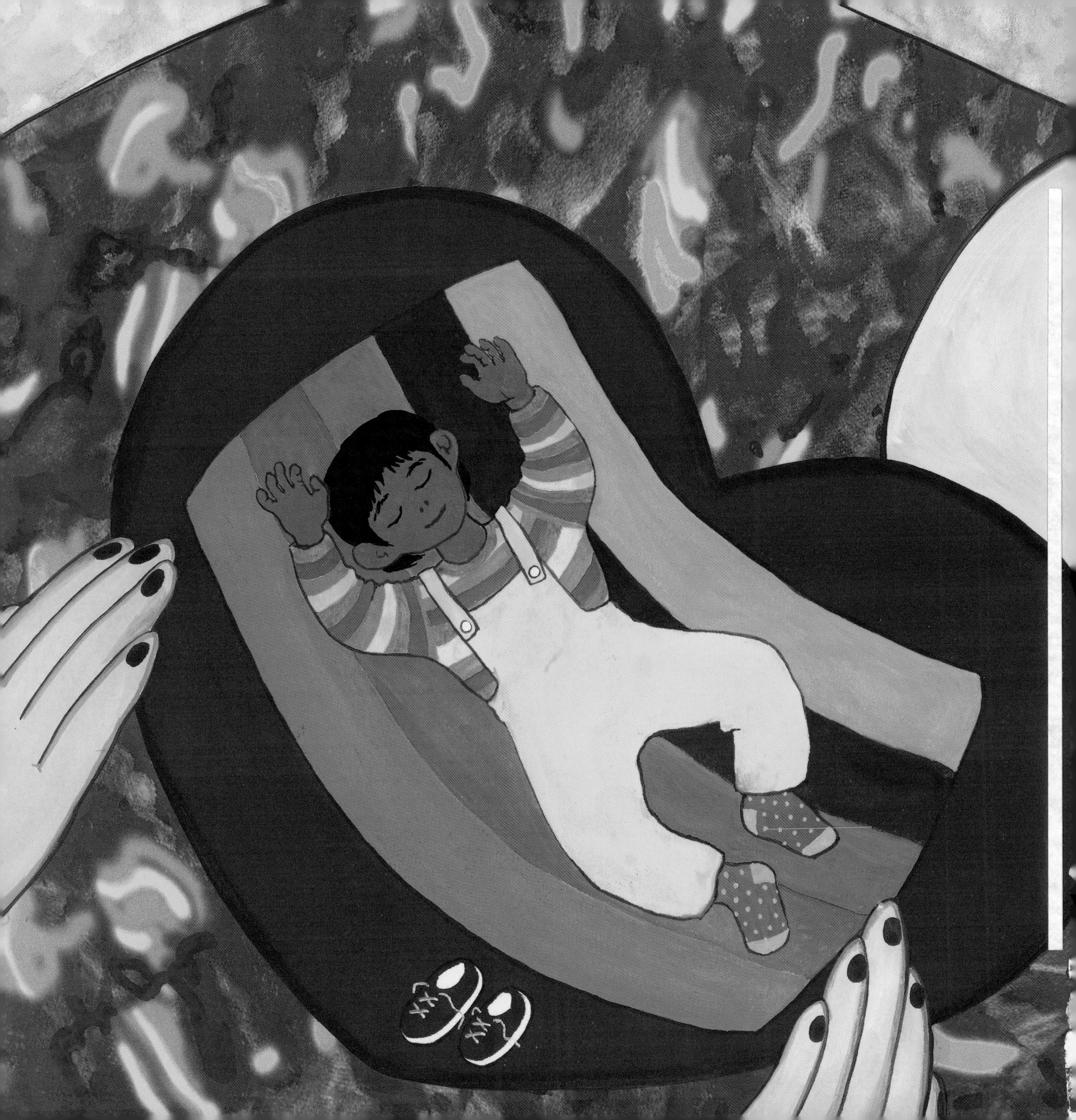

mmmm-

hmmm.

You got it.
Still here in my heart.

hen we're apart,
I miss you.

But then . . .

look inside my heart,
See you sitting there, and
Happy jumps right back in my front door.
ello
appy!

ou're with me in the worst weather, too.
When it's pouring rain
And the wind is blowing so hard
That all the umbrellas turn inside out,

r when it's as hot and dry as the desert at high noon . . .

Or when it's so dark and cold
That even penguins and polar bears
Hide their heads inside their chests and shiver,
Why, then—

feel you lying here all snug inside me,
Smiling your smile and asking,
"How's the weather out there?"
And I smile back and say,
"It's fine. It's just beautiful."

But when I come back home . . .

to ALL the SHIMANS
AAAAAAA

ater, when you've had your bath

nd put on your pajamas

nd brushed your teeth

nd are lying toasty warm in bed,

nd when you've finally fallen fast asleep,

then, do you know what?

Thanks to Andrea

You are STILL inside my heart.
How do you DO that,
always being in my heart?

And you know what else?
Guess who's always in that great big heart of YOURS?